green books for green readers

The Polar Bears' Home

A Story About Global Warming

By Lara Bergen

Illustrated by Vincent Nguyen

LITTLE SIMON

An imprint of Simon & Schuster Children's Publishing Division

New York London Toronto Sydney

1230 Avenue of the Americas, New York, New York 10020

Copyright © 2008 by Simon & Schuster, Inc.

LITTLE SIMON is a registered trademark of Simon & Schuster, Inc., and LITTLE GREEN BOOKS

and associated colophons are trademarks of Simon & Schuster, Inc.

Manufactured in the United States of America.

First Edition

2 4 6 8 10 9 7 5 3 1

ISBN-13: 978-1-4169-6787-3

ISBN-10: 1-4169-6787-7

Hello, welcome to the Arctic! Where I live, some things never change. In the summer the sun never sets. It is always light outside. And in the winter the sun never rises. It is dark all day!

But some things do change in the Arctic.
When I was little my dad would take me out on long dogsled rides
in the springtime. We would ride over the snowy land and frozen rivers
and see white Arctic hares and foxes and busy, little lemmings.

But this spring since so much snow and ice had melted, my dad said, "Let's go out for a boat ride instead."

And that's when I saw something I'd never seen before . . . two furry white balls on a sheet of ice, all alone.

"Look!" I called to my dad. "Look at those two dogs."

"Those aren't dogs," my dad told me. "Those are polar bear cubs. They look like they were born just this winter, and polar bear cubs like to stay close to their mother until they're almost three years old."

"Where is their mother?" I asked him.

"I don't know," said my dad. He was surprised too.

"In the fall," my dad explained, "when a mother polar bear's expecting a baby, she digs a cozy den in the snow, and there she stays until a little cub or twins are born a few months later."

"Is that when they come out?" I asked.

"Oh, no," said my dad. "New polar bears cubs are much too tiny—most weigh just a pound. They stay with their mother in their den until the springtime when they're big enough, like these cubs, to go outside and explore."

"And what about their father?"

"The polar bears' father does not sleep in the den with the mother and their cubs," said my dad. "Their father keeps hunting all winter."

"Of course, by then," my dad explained, "the polar bear mother hasn't eaten for months and months. And so it's just about this time of year that she heads out to the pack ice."

"Why do they head out to the pack ice?" I asked him.

"Because," he told me, "that's where the seals are, and that's what polar bears eat."

"I'm sure the mother of these cubs was thin and hungry after so many months in her den on shore," my dad said. "She was eager to take her cubs out where she could hunt seals and start teaching them how to hunt too."

Then my dad looked around at the icy sea and shook his head.

"I think the ice melted too fast this spring for this family. The mother probably left her cubs to watch her while she hunted, then the ice under the cubs broke off and carried them away."

"I thought polar bears could swim," I said. "Why didn't they swim back to her?"

"Polar bears are very good swimmers," my dad replied, "even in this freezing water. But these cubs are still too young. Their mother hasn't taught them yet."

"Maybe we should take the cubs home and take care of them," I said.

"I don't think so," my dad told me. "When these bears grow up, they will be *enormous*."

"Bigger than you?" I asked him.

"Much, much bigger," he said. "And they will need a lot of food that we just can't give them. Besides, polar bears are happiest living on the ice. Unlike other bears that hibernate in the winter, they stay busy when it's cold and slow down when it's warm."

"How do they keep warm in the winter?" I asked.

4 feet

1 foot

POLAR BEAR CUB

"Polar bears have a four-inch blanket of fat to keep them warm," my dad told me. "In fact they have to be careful not to get *overheated* when they run, even in the winter."

8 ½ feet

6 feet

MALE POLAR BEAR

"Unfortunately for polar bears," my dad said, "and many other animals, too, the Arctic is warming up more and more every year."

"Why?" I asked.

"The world and its climate are changing," he told me, "and we humans are making it change faster. We use a lot of energy—to heat our houses and run our factories, and even to power this boat—and most of it comes from burning oil and coal. That makes a gas which forms a tent around the earth and traps in extra heat."

"Polar bears aren't made for extra heat," he said. "A shorter winter means a shorter hunting season. It means less ice to hunt on and much more water to swim through to get to the ice."

"Will they be able to catch enough seals then?" I asked.

"Probably not," my dad said. "In fact the polar bears are already suffering. Many grown-up polar bears are not as healthy, and fewer cubs are born and survive every year."

My dad looked sad. "I've heard people say that if we don't try to help our planet now, there might be no more ice at all here in the Arctic when you grow up . . . and no more polar bears, either."

"Then we have to save these cubs!" I said.

"I'm not sure *we* can," said my dad. Then he brightened. "And maybe we don't have to."

He pointed to something white floating toward them in the water. Was it a small block of ice? No. It was the polar bear cubs' mother!

"Look!" I said, as she climbed up onto the ice floe and helped the cubs onto her back. "She's saving them herself!"

The next thing we knew, the mother was diving back into the water, with her cubs riding piggyback, and swimming smoothly toward the pack ice in the distance.

"Let's follow them!" I said.

When they reached the ice, the mother bear climbed up and sat down in the snow, and right away her cubs began nursing.

I was happy for them . . . but still a little worried.

"Will they be okay?" I asked my dad.

"I think so," he said. "But summer is coming and the ice is melting more each day. This mother bear has to get enough to eat while the ice is still here to be able to make milk for her cubs all through the summer." He grinned. "I think she looks like she can do it! But," he went on, "there are a lot more polar bears that will need our help from now on."

We can *all* help the polar bears. Here are some things *you* can do to slow down global warming:

Recycle aluminum cans, glass bottles, plastic, and cardboard.

Plant a tree. It will help clean the air and shade the earth.

Turn off things like the TV, computer, and lights when you're not using them, and even unplug them if you can.